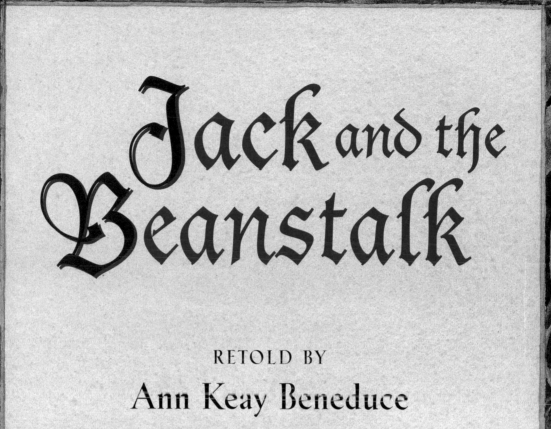

Jack and the Beanstalk

RETOLD BY

Ann Keay Beneduce

ILLUSTRATED BY

Gennady Spirin

PHILOMEL BOOKS • NEW YORK

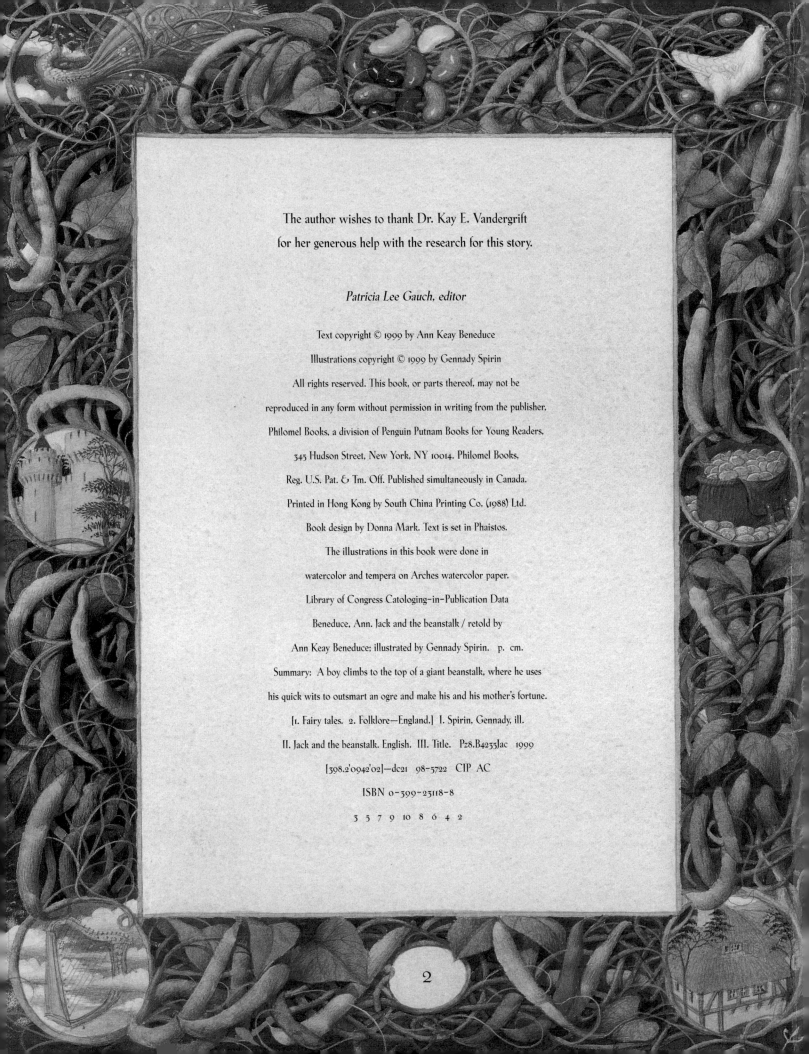

The author wishes to thank Dr. Kay E. Vandergrift
for her generous help with the research for this story.

Patricia Lee Gauch, editor

Text copyright © 1999 by Ann Keay Beneduce

Illustrations copyright © 1999 by Gennady Spirin

Philomel Books, a division of Penguin Putnam Books for Young Readers,

345 Hudson Street, New York, NY 10014. Philomel Books,

Reg. U.S. Pat. & Tm. Off. Published simultaneously in Canada.

Printed in Hong Kong by South China Printing Co. (1988) Ltd.

Book design by Donna Mark. Text is set in Phaistos.

The illustrations in this book were done in

watercolor and tempera on Arches watercolor paper.

Library of Congress Cataloging-in-Publication Data

Beneduce, Ann. Jack and the beanstalk / retold by

Ann Keay Beneduce; illustrated by Gennady Spirin.   p. cm.

Summary: A boy climbs to the top of a giant beanstalk, where he uses

his quick wits to outsmart an ogre and make his and his mother's fortune.

[1. Fairy tales. 2. Folklore—England.] I. Spirin, Gennady, ill.

II. Jack and the beanstalk. English. III. Title. Pz8.B4255Jac 1999

[398.2'0942'02]—dc21 98-5722 CIP AC

ISBN 0-399-23118-8

3 5 7 9 10 8 6 4 2

For Joel
—A.K.B.

For everyone who loves fairy tales
—G.S.

nce, in the days of good Queen Bess, there was a boy named Jack. He lived with his mother, a poor widow, in a little farmhouse not far from London. Jack was a lively, likable lad, but if he had one fault it was his curiosity. A closed gate was an open invitation to Jack; a tall fence was no obstacle, either, and he had followed every path in the forest to its end. He was always asking "What if...?" and "Why?" and "Where...?"

"What's for supper?" Jack asked his mother one evening.

"Oh, Jack, there isn't a bite to eat in the house," she replied. "And we haven't a penny left to buy more. Whatever shall we do?" The poor woman threw her apron over her head and began to sob.

"Don't worry, Mother," said Jack. "I'll take care of you. I'll find a job."

"A job!" she exclaimed. "Who would hire a little boy like you? You've a kind heart, but you are much too young to find work."

"Well, then," said Jack, "what choice do we have? We'll have to sell Milky White, our dear old cow. She doesn't give us much milk these days, anyhow. Tomorrow I'll take her to the market, and I'll get a good price for her, too. Everything will be all right, you'll see!"

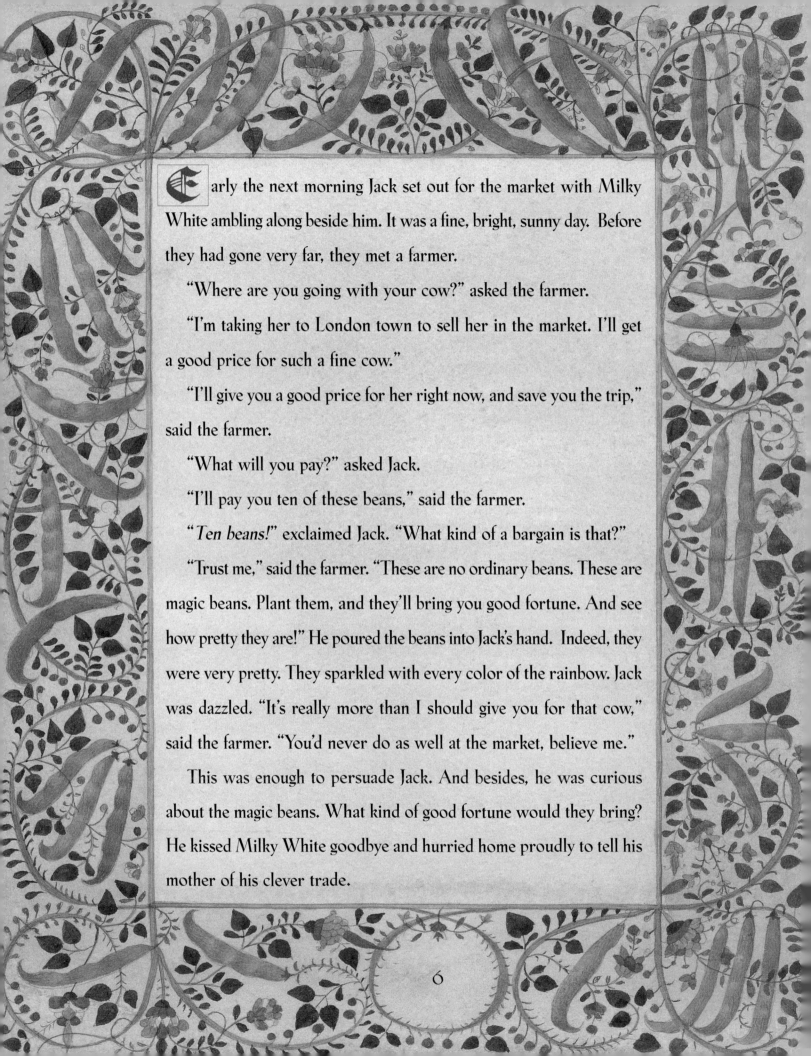

Early the next morning Jack set out for the market with Milky White ambling along beside him. It was a fine, bright, sunny day. Before they had gone very far, they met a farmer.

"Where are you going with your cow?" asked the farmer.

"I'm taking her to London town to sell her in the market. I'll get a good price for such a fine cow."

"I'll give you a good price for her right now, and save you the trip," said the farmer.

"What will you pay?" asked Jack.

"I'll pay you ten of these beans," said the farmer.

"*Ten beans!*" exclaimed Jack. "What kind of a bargain is that?"

"Trust me," said the farmer. "These are no ordinary beans. These are magic beans. Plant them, and they'll bring you good fortune. And see how pretty they are!" He poured the beans into Jack's hand. Indeed, they were very pretty. They sparkled with every color of the rainbow. Jack was dazzled. "It's really more than I should give you for that cow," said the farmer. "You'd never do as well at the market, believe me."

This was enough to persuade Jack. And besides, he was curious about the magic beans. What kind of good fortune would they bring? He kissed Milky White goodbye and hurried home proudly to tell his mother of his clever trade.

h, Jack, what a foolish boy you are!" she exclaimed. "You have sold our good cow for nothing but a handful of worthless beans!" She tossed the beans right out of the window and sent Jack supperless to bed.

The next morning, Jack awoke first. He noticed something strange outside the window of their small home.

"Mother! Mother! Wake up!" he shouted. "Look out the window! The beans really are magic! They've grown right up to the sky!"

Sure enough, the beans had grown. Their great thick stems had twined and looped and wound around one another, forming a sort of ladder that reached all the way up into the clouds. Whatever could be up there?

"I'm going to climb up the beanstalk," Jack announced.

"Oh, no, don't go," cried his mother. "I'm afraid something bad will happen to you."

But Jack was already on his way.

p and up he climbed until finally he reached the top. He looked around in wonder. He was in a forest of ancient trees whose twisted trunks looked like wizened old men. Jack was a little scared but, seeing a path, he set out along it.

He had not gone far when he saw a beautiful woman ahead of him. She was dressed all in white and carried a wand with a golden peacock at its tip. The wand shone with a gently glimmering light. Who could she be? Jack went straight up to her, but before he could ask her any questions, she spoke.

"I've been waiting for you, Jack," she said, smiling.

"How did you know my name?" Jack asked.

She answered with another question: "Do you remember your father, Jack?"

"No, ma'am," he replied. "My mother just weeps when I ask what happened to him, and says she cannot talk about it."

"But I can," replied the beautiful woman. "I am a fairy and was your father's guardian. But my magical powers were taken away from me for several years, so I wasn't able to help him when he needed me most." The fairy looked so sad that Jack had to beg her to go on.

I will, but you must promise to do exactly what I tell you, or you will meet the same fate as your father."

Jack gave her his word.

"Your father was a kind, loving, generous man. He had a good wife, a fine house, a newborn son—yourself—and plenty of money. But he also had a false friend—a giant. This wicked creature killed your father and stole all his riches. The giant warned your poor mother never to tell you anything about your father or how he died, or he would murder her, and you, too. Then he sent her away, with you in her arms. I couldn't help her either, as I got back my magical powers only yesterday—the day you sold your cow.

"That farmer cheated you," she went on. "Those were just ordinary beans. It was I who made that enormous beanstalk grow from them and who inspired you to climb it, for this is where the evil giant lives. It is up to you to avenge your father and to take back what is rightfully yours. But you must never tell your mother that you have learned anything about your father. The giant is still very dangerous."

"I promise," said Jack. "But where does the giant live?"

"Just follow this road. And be a brave boy," replied the fairy. Then she smiled again, and vanished.

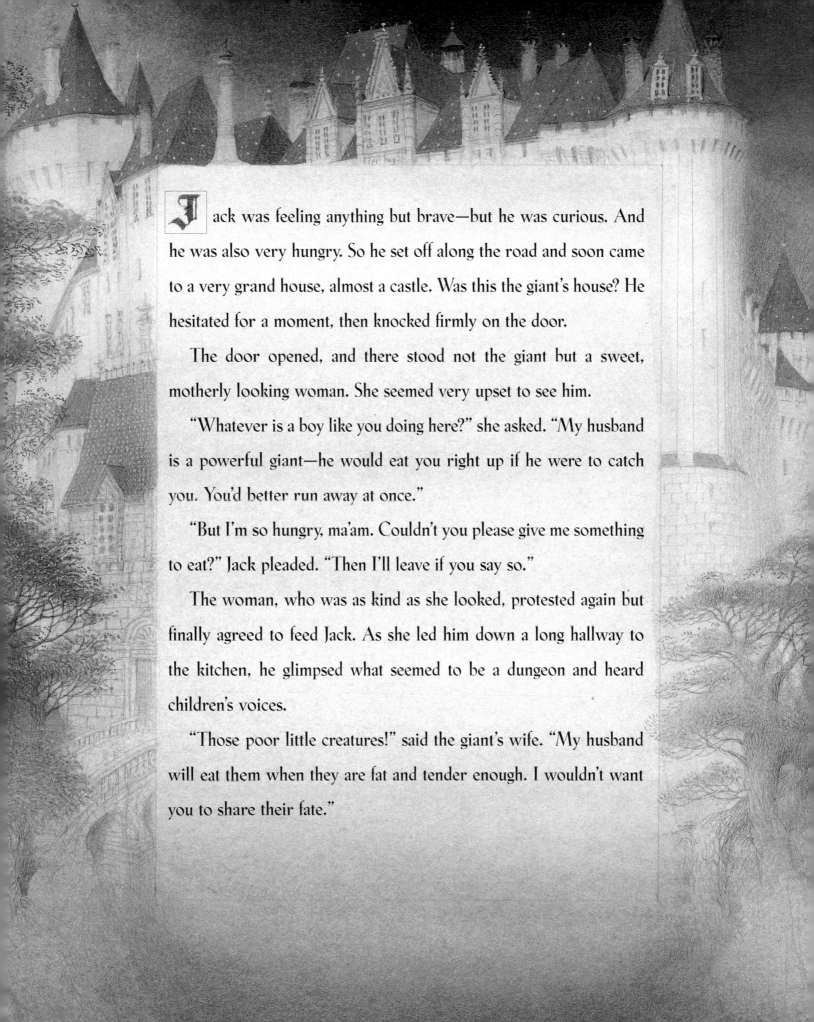

Jack was feeling anything but brave—but he was curious. And he was also very hungry. So he set off along the road and soon came to a very grand house, almost a castle. Was this the giant's house? He hesitated for a moment, then knocked firmly on the door.

The door opened, and there stood not the giant but a sweet, motherly looking woman. She seemed very upset to see him.

"Whatever is a boy like you doing here?" she asked. "My husband is a powerful giant—he would eat you right up if he were to catch you. You'd better run away at once."

"But I'm so hungry, ma'am. Couldn't you please give me something to eat?" Jack pleaded. "Then I'll leave if you say so."

The woman, who was as kind as she looked, protested again but finally agreed to feed Jack. As she led him down a long hallway to the kitchen, he glimpsed what seemed to be a dungeon and heard children's voices.

"Those poor little creatures!" said the giant's wife. "My husband will eat them when they are fat and tender enough. I wouldn't want you to share their fate."

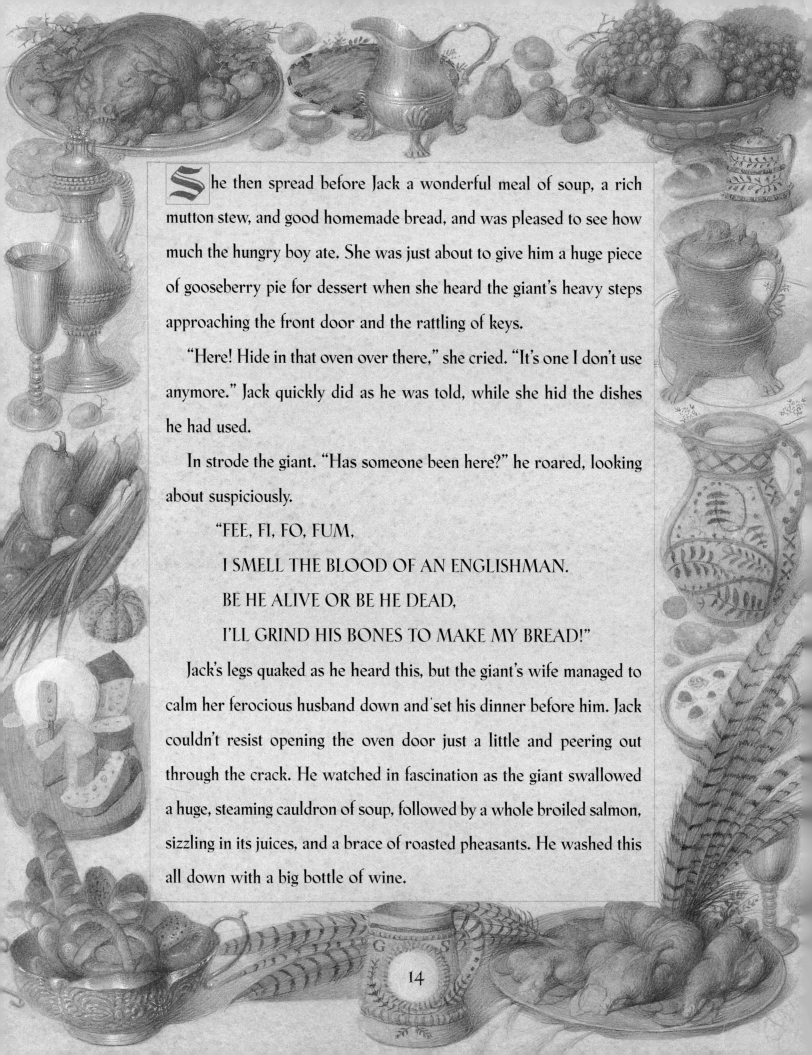

She then spread before Jack a wonderful meal of soup, a rich mutton stew, and good homemade bread, and was pleased to see how much the hungry boy ate. She was just about to give him a huge piece of gooseberry pie for dessert when she heard the giant's heavy steps approaching the front door and the rattling of keys.

"Here! Hide in that oven over there," she cried. "It's one I don't use anymore." Jack quickly did as he was told, while she hid the dishes he had used.

In strode the giant. "Has someone been here?" he roared, looking about suspiciously.

"FEE, FI, FO, FUM,

I SMELL THE BLOOD OF AN ENGLISHMAN.

BE HE ALIVE OR BE HE DEAD,

I'LL GRIND HIS BONES TO MAKE MY BREAD!"

Jack's legs quaked as he heard this, but the giant's wife managed to calm her ferocious husband down and set his dinner before him. Jack couldn't resist opening the oven door just a little and peering out through the crack. He watched in fascination as the giant swallowed a huge, steaming cauldron of soup, followed by a whole broiled salmon, sizzling in its juices, and a brace of roasted pheasants. He washed this all down with a big bottle of wine.

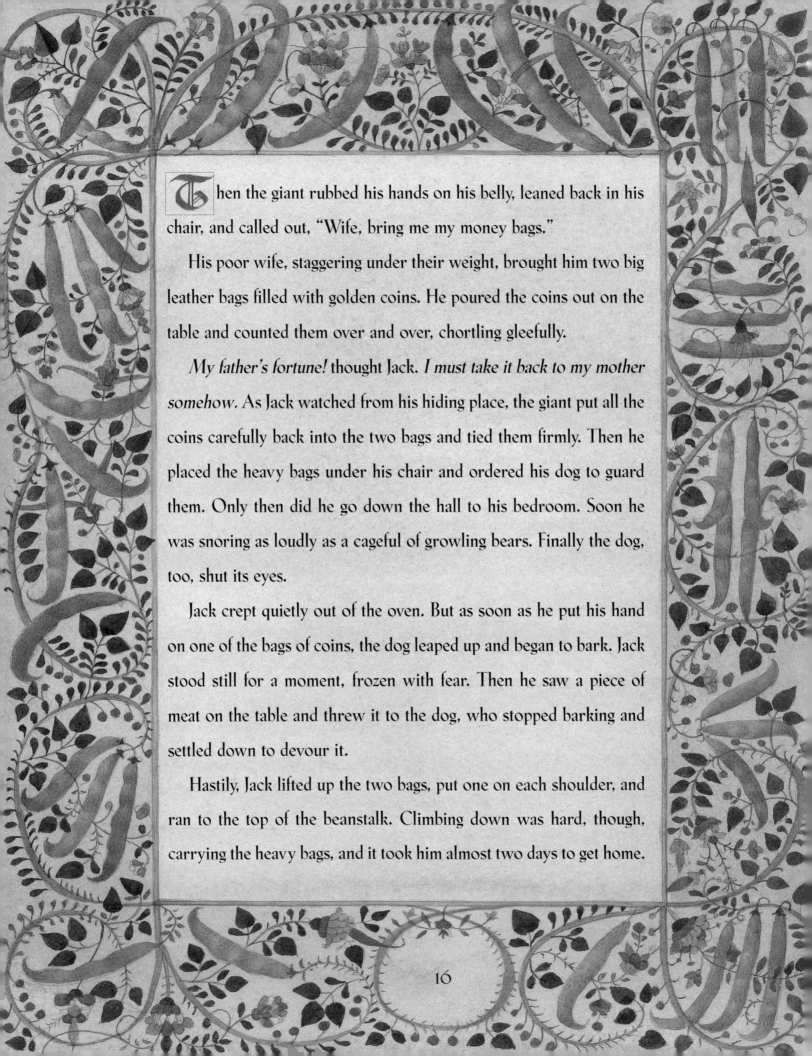

Then the giant rubbed his hands on his belly, leaned back in his chair, and called out, "Wife, bring me my money bags."

His poor wife, staggering under their weight, brought him two big leather bags filled with golden coins. He poured the coins out on the table and counted them over and over, chortling gleefully.

My father's fortune! thought Jack. *I must take it back to my mother somehow.* As Jack watched from his hiding place, the giant put all the coins carefully back into the two bags and tied them firmly. Then he placed the heavy bags under his chair and ordered his dog to guard them. Only then did he go down the hall to his bedroom. Soon he was snoring as loudly as a cageful of growling bears. Finally the dog, too, shut its eyes.

Jack crept quietly out of the oven. But as soon as he put his hand on one of the bags of coins, the dog leaped up and began to bark. Jack stood still for a moment, frozen with fear. Then he saw a piece of meat on the table and threw it to the dog, who stopped barking and settled down to devour it.

Hastily, Jack lifted up the two bags, put one on each shoulder, and ran to the top of the beanstalk. Climbing down was hard, though, carrying the heavy bags, and it took him almost two days to get home.

16

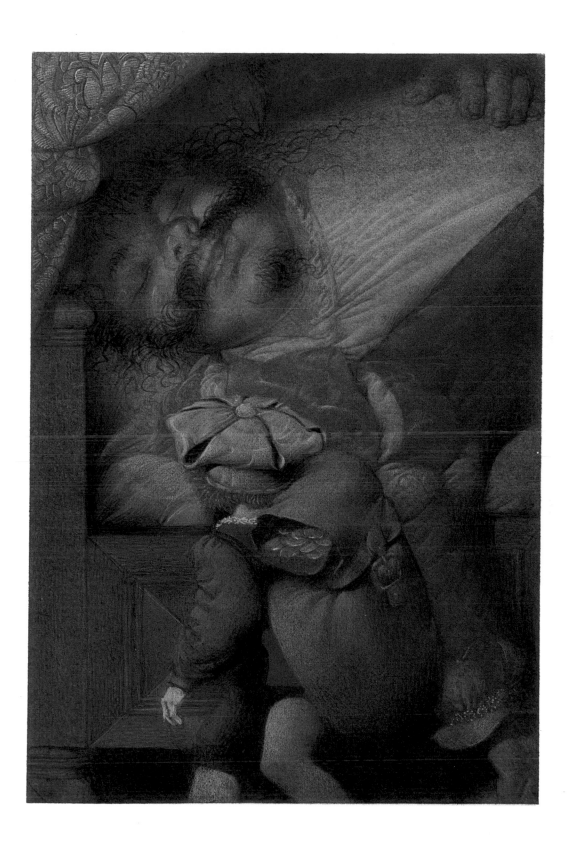

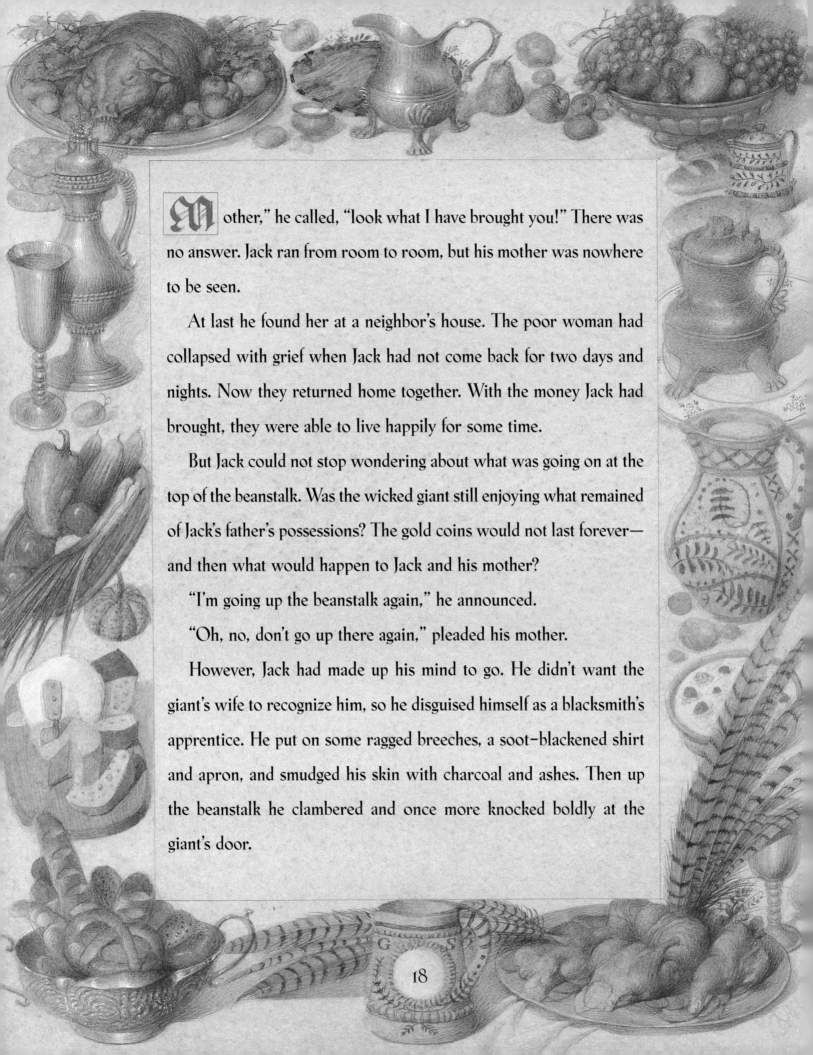

Mother," he called, "look what I have brought you!" There was no answer. Jack ran from room to room, but his mother was nowhere to be seen.

At last he found her at a neighbor's house. The poor woman had collapsed with grief when Jack had not come back for two days and nights. Now they returned home together. With the money Jack had brought, they were able to live happily for some time.

But Jack could not stop wondering about what was going on at the top of the beanstalk. Was the wicked giant still enjoying what remained of Jack's father's possessions? The gold coins would not last forever—and then what would happen to Jack and his mother?

"I'm going up the beanstalk again," he announced.

"Oh, no, don't go up there again," pleaded his mother.

However, Jack had made up his mind to go. He didn't want the giant's wife to recognize him, so he disguised himself as a blacksmith's apprentice. He put on some ragged breeches, a soot-blackened shirt and apron, and smudged his skin with charcoal and ashes. Then up the beanstalk he clambered and once more knocked boldly at the giant's door.

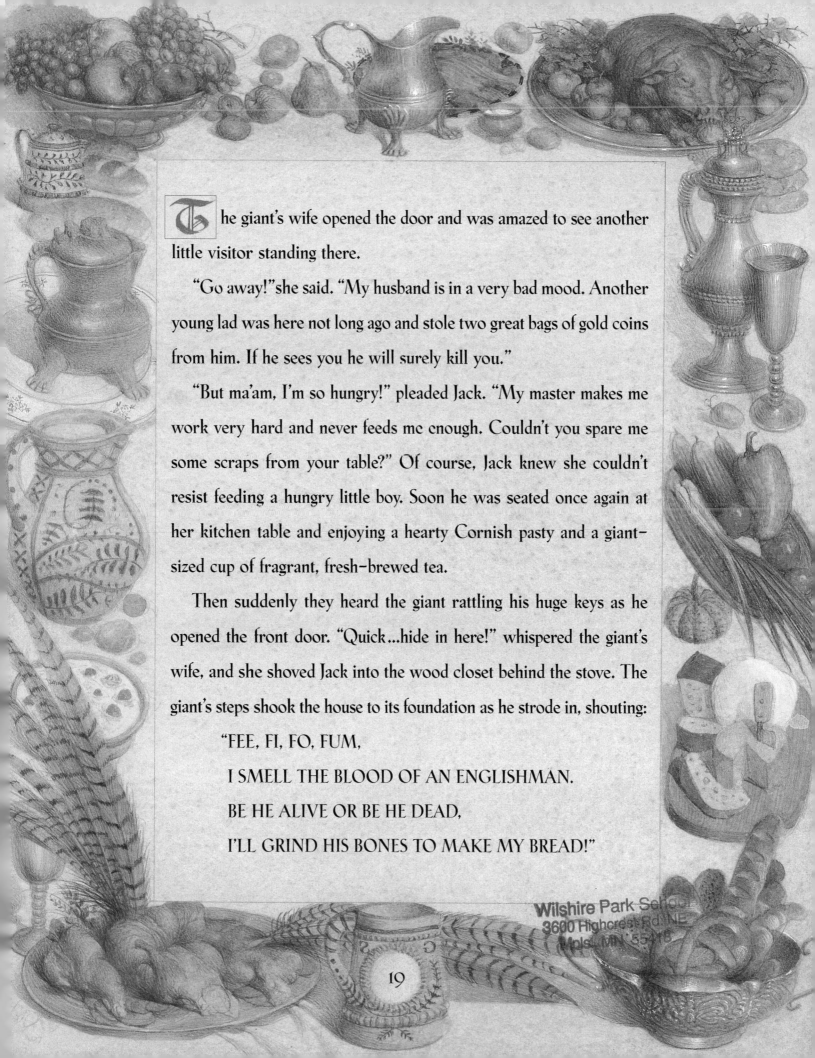

The giant's wife opened the door and was amazed to see another little visitor standing there.

"Go away!" she said. "My husband is in a very bad mood. Another young lad was here not long ago and stole two great bags of gold coins from him. If he sees you he will surely kill you."

"But ma'am, I'm so hungry!" pleaded Jack. "My master makes me work very hard and never feeds me enough. Couldn't you spare me some scraps from your table?" Of course, Jack knew she couldn't resist feeding a hungry little boy. Soon he was seated once again at her kitchen table and enjoying a hearty Cornish pasty and a giant-sized cup of fragrant, fresh-brewed tea.

Then suddenly they heard the giant rattling his huge keys as he opened the front door. "Quick...hide in here!" whispered the giant's wife, and she shoved Jack into the wood closet behind the stove. The giant's steps shook the house to its foundation as he strode in, shouting:

"FEE, FI, FO, FUM,

I SMELL THE BLOOD OF AN ENGLISHMAN.

BE HE ALIVE OR BE HE DEAD,

I'LL GRIND HIS BONES TO MAKE MY BREAD!"

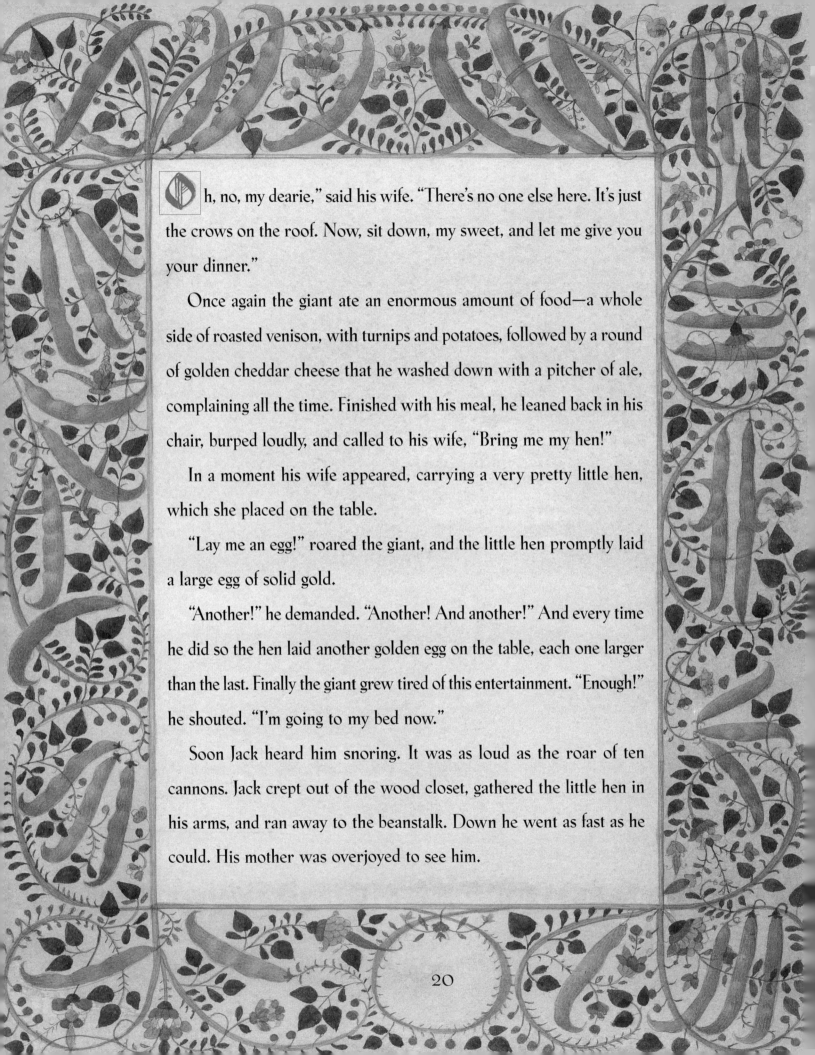

h, no, my dearie," said his wife. "There's no one else here. It's just the crows on the roof. Now, sit down, my sweet, and let me give you your dinner."

Once again the giant ate an enormous amount of food—a whole side of roasted venison, with turnips and potatoes, followed by a round of golden cheddar cheese that he washed down with a pitcher of ale, complaining all the time. Finished with his meal, he leaned back in his chair, burped loudly, and called to his wife, "Bring me my hen!"

In a moment his wife appeared, carrying a very pretty little hen, which she placed on the table.

"Lay me an egg!" roared the giant, and the little hen promptly laid a large egg of solid gold.

"Another!" he demanded. "Another! And another!" And every time he did so the hen laid another golden egg on the table, each one larger than the last. Finally the giant grew tired of this entertainment. "Enough!" he shouted. "I'm going to my bed now."

Soon Jack heard him snoring. It was as loud as the roar of ten cannons. Jack crept out of the wood closet, gathered the little hen in his arms, and ran away to the beanstalk. Down he went as fast as he could. His mother was overjoyed to see him.

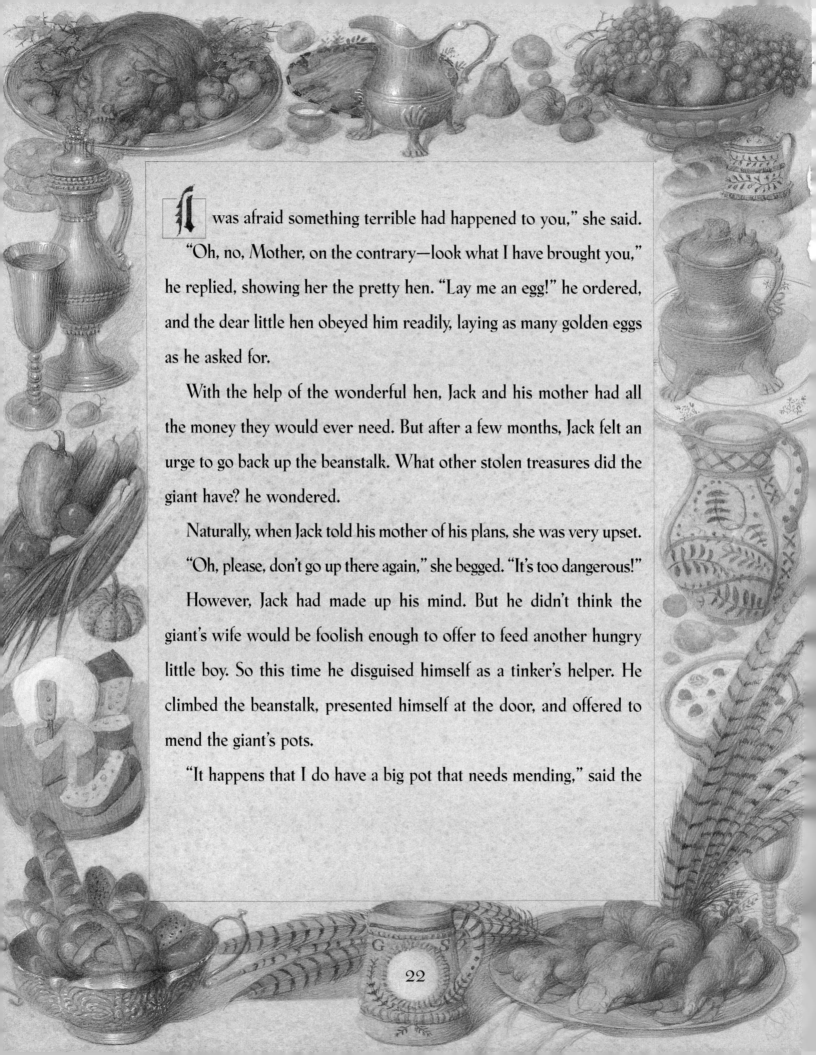

I was afraid something terrible had happened to you," she said.

"Oh, no, Mother, on the contrary—look what I have brought you," he replied, showing her the pretty hen. "Lay me an egg!" he ordered, and the dear little hen obeyed him readily, laying as many golden eggs as he asked for.

With the help of the wonderful hen, Jack and his mother had all the money they would ever need. But after a few months, Jack felt an urge to go back up the beanstalk. What other stolen treasures did the giant have? he wondered.

Naturally, when Jack told his mother of his plans, she was very upset.

"Oh, please, don't go up there again," she begged. "It's too dangerous!"

However, Jack had made up his mind. But he didn't think the giant's wife would be foolish enough to offer to feed another hungry little boy. So this time he disguised himself as a tinker's helper. He climbed the beanstalk, presented himself at the door, and offered to mend the giant's pots.

"It happens that I do have a big pot that needs mending," said the giant's wife, and she led Jack to the kitchen, where she showed him an enormous copper pot with two holes in the bottom. Jack jumped inside and was pretending to mend the holes when the giant returned. Quickly, the giant's wife put the lid on the great copper pot, and at first Jack felt quite safe in there, until the giant strode into the kitchen, shouting:

> "FEE, FI, FO, FUM,
>
> I SMELL THE BLOOD OF AN ENGLISHMAN.
>
> BE HE ALIVE OR BE HE DEAD,
>
> I'LL GRIND HIS BONES TO MAKE MY BREAD!"

Then he put his huge hand on the lid of the copper pot as if to lift it. Jack was sure his last moment had come.

But just then the giant's wife spoke. "Come, my dear," she said. "It's only your dinner that you smell. It's ready right now."

So the giant did not bother to lift the lid after all, but sat down at the big table by the fireside. Jack was too frightened this time to peek out and see what he was eating.

When he finished his huge meal, the giant leaned back in his chair once again, wiped his greasy beard with his fingers, and commanded his wife to bring in his harp. Now Jack could not resist lifting the lid a little. On the table before him stood a beautiful little harp. As Jack watched, the giant said, "Play!" and the harp played the most exquisite music imaginable, without anybody touching it. Jack was enchanted, and was more determined to get this than any of the giant's treasures.

The giant was soon lulled into a stupor by the harp's music and went off to bed early, followed by his wife. When he thought it was safe, Jack got out of the pot, seized the harp, and started to run off with it. But the harp, finding itself in strange hands, began calling loudly, *"Master! Master!"*

The giant awoke and saw Jack scampering away as fast as his legs could carry him.

"Oh, you little villain! It must have been you who made off with my hen and my money bags—and now you have taken my magic harp. I will catch you and eat you alive!" he shouted.

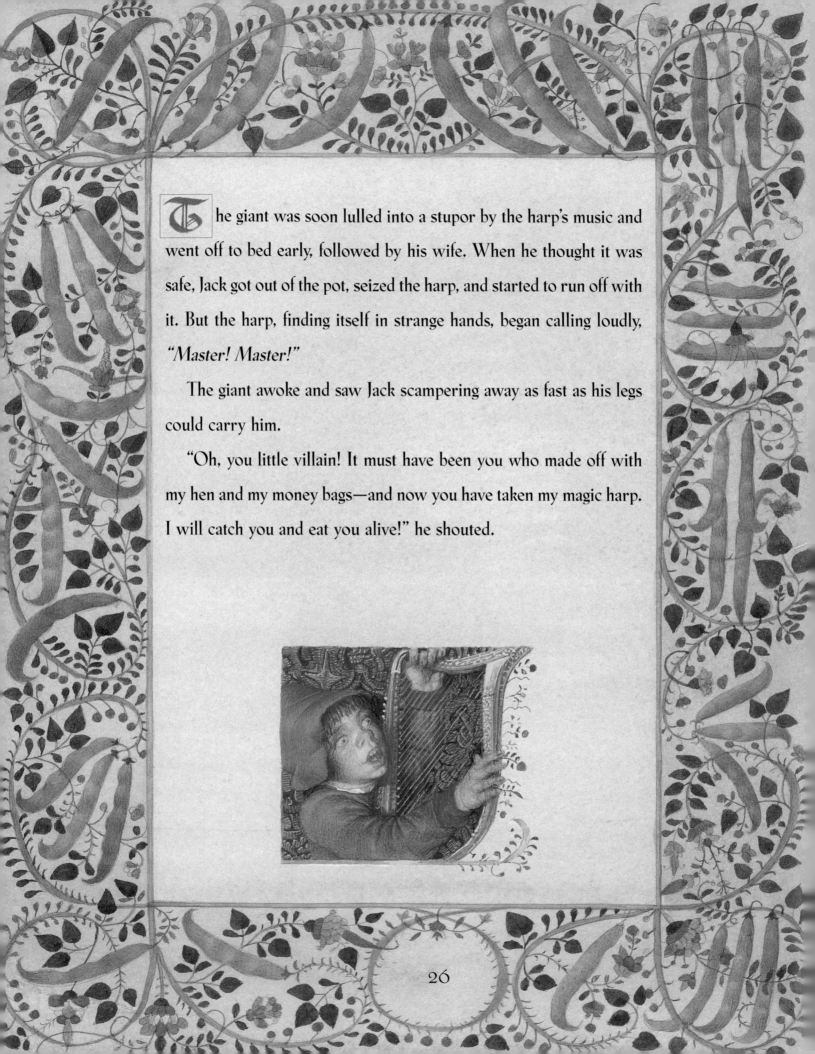

ut Jack had young legs and a clear conscience, which gave him an advantage over the giant, who was still rather drowsy after being awakened so suddenly. So Jack beat him quite easily in a race to the beanstalk and slid down quickly. At the bottom, he found his mother sitting in the doorway and weeping.

uickly, Mother," called Jack. "Don't cry; just hand me my hatchet. Please *hurry!*" He looked up and saw the giant stepping onto the top of the beanstalk. The huge monster was halfway down before Jack finally managed to hack through the beanstalk near its root. The whole beanstalk twisted…swayed…and then *crashed* to the ground, carrying the wicked giant down with it. And that was the end of the giant and his evil deeds. Everyone in the countryside rejoiced.

Now that the giant was gone, the good fairy was able to explain everything to Jack's mother. Jack and his mother lived happily until the end of their days. Nothing more was ever heard or seen of the land at the top of the magical beanstalk. But Jack often wondered about it.